By the Glow of the Strawberry Moon

ISBN **978-1-947514-55-3**

Printed in the United States of America
St. Clair Publications
P. O. Box 726
Mc Minnville, TN 37111-0726

http://stclairpublications.com

Cover design by Spencer St. Clair

Lockwood House, Harpers Ferry, National Park Service, page 6
https://www.nps.gov/hafe/learn/historyculture/lockwood-house.htm

By the Glow of the Strawberry Moon

Stanley J. St. Clair

Inspired by actual events

StCP

Disclaimer:

Although the basic theme of this story is inspired by true events, all names, places and incidents are a work of fiction and exist only in the imagination of the author.

Notice: Contains racial slurs. Some language is not suitable for children under 18.

Other books by Stanley J. St. Clair inspired by actual events are:

Conspiracy in the Town that Time Forgot
ISBN 978-0-9801704-9-8
True Crime Drama, 2009, St. Clair Publications

Quinn ISBN 978-0-9801704-7-4
Family Historic Novella based on a True Story, 2009, St. Clair Publications

Beyond the Thistle Patch ISBN 978-1-935786-03-0
Memoirs of Youth, 2010, St. Clair Publications

Turning Point at Gettysburg
ISBN 978-1-947514-31-7 Paperback;
978-1-947514-35-5 Hardcover
Civil War Historic Novel Based on a True Story, 2021, St. Clair Publications

They Call it Treason ISBN 978-1-947514-33-1
Paperback; **978-1-947514-41-6** Hardcover
American Revolutionary War Historic Novel
Based on a True Story, 2021, St. Clair Publications

The Black Widow of Hazel Green
ISBN 978-1-947514-43-0 Paperback
978-1-947514-44-7 Hardcover
19th Century Historic Novel Based on a True Story, 2022, St. Clair Publications

Chapter 1

I swore I would never write this story because of the devastating effect it could have on my family and me. But last week, when I was diagnosed with an inoperable malignant brain tumor, I felt compelled to put on paper this macabre account for the world to read. I've shared the news of my diagnosis with no one but my darling wife, Annette. She was extremely distressed, and wanted to tell our three children and our grandchildren, but I asked her indulgence until I could inform them in the proper manner.

I only have a few months left to write this story, so I'm going to get started. It's been thirty years since this terrible saga ended, and I've kept these memories all bottled up inside me. The more I deliberated on it, the more I remembered, and the more I became determined to come clean with it.

The Blair clan was one of the Virginia Colony's first families. We are of the Scottish Clan Blair from Perthshire. Even in the old homeland, our ancestors married into prominent families and became powerful in their own right.

My uncle, Jacob Blair, and his third-cousin wife, Hazel, lived in a tall, white-columned Colonial mansion on a charming grassy knoll at the southwest edge of the city of Roanoke. The 150 acre remnant of the once sprawling Blair Plantation had been inherited by Hazel when her father, affectionately known in the greater clan as "Uncle Christopher," had passed away in 1952. The city had annexed the entire estate in order to collect more taxes.

Jake and Hazel had married in a simple, unpretentious ceremony at the home in April, 1962. Neither of them was very religious. Theirs was obviously not a perfect relationship. Hazel was in her mid-fifties at the time of their nuptials and Jake was almost twenty years her junior. My father, Anson, and his other brothers just shook their heads. They thought Jake had lost his mind. But then my dad had plenty of land of his own, and raised Hereford cattle, which he dearly loved doing. The farm kept him occupied and he had no time to be critical of his younger brothers.

If asked what had brought them together, Jake and Hazel told everyone that they both felt they needed companionship. Of course Hazel was far past the age of bearing children, and was shy and had never been married. She had lived all alone in that gigantic house and keeping everything in the family seemed important to her. I know she was attracted to Uncle Jake's boyish good looks and broad smile.

Jake was from a long line of planters and farmers, so tending the farm came natural to him. He had hired some local descendants of slaves to help because he could get them to work so much cheaper than whites who wanted to "keep up with the Joneses."

Up until the past few years they had been autonomous and didn't seem to want family butting into their business, though rumor had it that they were becoming cross with one another after Hazel became totally bedfast with severe rheumatoid arthritis. For over three years she had been on heavy, regulated shots of morphine. She had been able, until the last several months, to give them to herself. She still likely could have, after they were prepared, but Jake had volunteered to administer them to make it easier on her.

I had graduated high school right after Uncle Jake and Aunt Hazel married then spent four years at Virginia Tech in Blacksburg before going to Washington and Lee and obtaining my Doctor of Judicial Science. I could have run for judge, and some of my friends encouraged it, but I preferred trying criminal cases. I guess I was always up for a challenge.

My dad and my mother, Trudy who was, at the time, a junior college professor were both so very proud of me! They would have paid my entire tuition, but it was not necessary. I was granted a four-year academic scholarship to Tech, and worked my way through law school. I was always independent, having earned my own way working at a grocery store from the time I entered high school to buy my own clothes, car, gas and other things I wanted for myself.

Being a trial attorney who was much in demand, I kept a busy schedule, but felt it my duty since Hazel had gotten so sick to go by the mansion at least once a month and see how they were faring. I would always make my visit late in the evening, due to my work.

My sister, Liz, owned a boutique in the mall and was dedicated to her customers and taking care of her husband and children, so she showed no interest in checking on Uncle Jake and Aunt Hazel.

Most of Jake's other brothers, other than my dad and Uncle Marty, had moved out of the area, and their children were scattered all over the East.

I had been blessed to have married the ideal soul mate in Annette Carter. I had met her in college and dated her until I finished law school before saying our 'I dos' in a most lavish wedding at First Presbyterian in Roanoke on Saturday, June 20, 1968. Annette is a direct descendant of Colonel Landon Carter of Revolutionary War fame, who was a celebrated planter and member of the Virginia House of Burgesses.

Annette took up medicine and became a general practitioner, while I was studying law.

I guess we spoiled our children, Robert II, Jonathan and Louisa, who came along one right after the other. Well, shoot, I know we did. They all three married well and became responsible, solid pillars of their communities. I guess I failed to mention my own name earlier. I'm Robert Louis Blair I, of course.

Chapter 2

"**G**ood morning Roanoke! We have breaking news this morning! Local wealthy recluse, Hazel Blair, was found unresponsive in her home in South Roanoke late last night. We have been told that Mrs. Blair was DOA at General Hospital. We will bring you more details as they become available. Her husband has been taken in to police headquarters for questioning. We have a reporter on the way to the scene."

It was Thursday, June 27, 1991. I had set my clock radio to awaken me at 6:00 AM. I shook my head to try to fully wake up. What on earth had happened? I dared not think of it! I had just been by their home the evening before. The lights had been out in the parlor but I had peeped in the front window and by the soft full moonlight saw Uncle Jake laying Aunt Hazel down on the sofa. She seemed to be sleeping, so I knew it was not a good time and left without saying a word. Something was a bit off, but I didn't know exactly what, for I only got a glance.

My mind seemed hazy as to exactly what I had witnessed. I swept it from my mind and decided to have a quick cup of java and drive to police headquarters. Why hadn't I been called? I was his nephew; but I was also his attorney.

I aroused Annette and related the horrible news to her.

"Do you want me to go with you?" she asked.

"No, I'll have to talk to him in confidence and there's nothing you can do. But thanks for offering."

I guzzled down my hot coffee and dashed to my Cadillac Fleetwood Brougham.

On the way to the station, anxious questions were buzzing through my troubled mind. "What really happened? What could have caused Aunt Hazel's death? Why was my kind uncle called in for questioning?"

When I arrived, Captain Doug Showalter spotted me before I got through the front door.

"Good morning Rob. So sorry about your aunt."

"Well, there's nothing more that can be done for her and she had been suffering for years. She was 83 years old, you know. How is Uncle Jake taking it?"

"From what I can surmise he's in shock. But he seems a little nervous to me."

"Well, I can certainly understand that! I'd be nervous too if my wife just died and I was being questioned by the cops. Why the blue blazes do you have him in here for questioning? And why wasn't I called?"

"It's just routine, Rob. You know the drill. When anyone is taking a dangerous drug and ends up dead we have to question the spouse. After all, he was the only one there with her last night."

"When was he brought in?"

"About 2:00 this morning, I was told. I just got here a few minutes ago."

"Well, I want to see him now!"

"Sure, Rob," and he opened the door to the interrogation room where the Chief was giving Jake the third degree.

"Uncle Jake, I'm so very sorry about Aunt Hazel!"

I turned to Police Chief Larry Watts. "I want to talk to my uncle alone, please. Why didn't you call me? Was he read his Miranda rights?"

"Of course, Rob! We run a tight ship here! But he said he hadn't done anything wrong and didn't need a lawyer."

After the door was closed, I looked my uncle square in the eye.

"I came by your place last night right after dark. All the lights were out in the front of your house and I don't think you heard me. My car is quiet and I parked a ways from your door. You and Aunt Hazel were still up. I saw you laying her down on the couch and kissing her forehead. I don't believe you did anything wrong. Can you just tell me exactly what happened?"

"Sure, Robbie. I had just given Hazel her evening shot and was getting ready to take her to bed. We were both really worn out. I had been working around the house and neither of us had a nap yesterday. She shut her eyes, so I laid her head back on a cushion on the sofa. I was going to carry her to bed. I sat down on the easy chair next to her and nodded off. It must have been an hour later when I woke up and put my hands under her. You know that she had a downstairs bedroom because of her condition."

"Sure, I knew that. I've gone in there a few times to see her."

"When I started to pick her up, I could tell she wasn't breathing. I checked for her pulse. I didn't feel one. That's when I felt that she was turning cold. I grabbed the phone and called 9-1-1. The paramedics took her to the hospital where she was pronounced dead on arrival."

Uncle Jake broke down in tears. He was wiping his eyes with his handkerchief. I could tell he was truly torn up over her passing.

"I'm sure that they can tell everything is as you say, Uncle Jake. I'll ask Larry if I can take you to our house."

"There will be an ongoing investigation, Rob," Larry said as we left. "We will have to get a coroner's report as to the most likely cause of her death. Jake, I'm truly sorry about your wife. Just stay close. We may need to talk to you again."

Chapter 3

Uncle Jake fell asleep on the way to our house. Not getting any rest the night before had been rough on him. Although he was only 64 years old, he was a bad diabetic and had severe heart trouble.

I asked him about his medications when I got him into the guest room; then while he slept, I drove to his house and picked them up, as well as a change of clothes for him.

Annette had left me a note and gone on to her office, because she had patients coming in starting at 8:30.

I called my office and told my law partner, Allen Arbuckle that I was taking the day off to be with Uncle Jake.

I went into the living room and turned on HBO, hoping I could find a good murder mystery to get my mind off the situation at hand. But it darn sure didn't work! I couldn't think about any other mystery when there was a whale of a big one starring me in the face.

I laid back in my Lazy Boy and an old Glenn Campbell song started running through my head over and over: Gentle on My Mind. Even that didn't seem gentle. I gritted my teeth. I wrinkled my brow and moaned.

My thoughts trailed off like a frightened child lost in the dark Virginia woods on a sultry night. My imagination was running rampant. I knew there had been something I couldn't recall from the night before, but what? I am one-track minded and had been concentrating on my uncle kissing my aunt's forehead.

Maybe I was overreacting, I thought. But I figured Uncle Jake didn't realize how serious his position seemed to law enforcement.

In the distance to the east I heard the mournful wail of a siren. It sounded like an ambulance to my trained ear.

The phone rang and startled me. It was Annette.

"What happened at the station, Honey? Is Uncle Jake alright? I called your office and your secretary told me you were at home."

I filled her in on the details of everything that went on that morning and told her about bringing Jake home with me.

"I'm waiting on a call from Larry about the coroner's report. He said it wouldn't be long."

"I can feel your stress, Rob. Don't get yourself all in a tizzy over this. Heart problems run in your family, you know. What happened, happened. There's nothing you can do to change it. I guess you'll need to help Uncle Jake with the funeral arrangements."

I hadn't thought about that, but it was a fact. In his shape he couldn't do it on his own. I knew he was uneducated and hadn't had to deal with death before. He had lived a sheltered life growing up on Grandpa's farm.

"I know, my dear. I won't get too stressed." But I already was.

I tuned in some soft music on the stereo. I lay down again on the leather recliner and pushed my head backward. It had only been about twenty minutes or so when the phone rang again.

"Blair residence, Rob speaking."

"Hey Rob. It's Larry. I got the coroner's report."

"And?"

"And you need to come in. I want to talk to you before we take this any further."

"What about my uncle? He's sleeping."

"Leave him a note. Just tell him something came up and you'll be back soon."

I did as he suggested and slowly closed the door as I left.

Chapter 4

"**D**r. Patel said that Hazel's death was almost certainly from an overdose of morphine. He has sent for a toxicology report. Jake admitted to giving her the last shot. I'm sending some officers out to the house to see what they can find."

Oh, my God! I thought. *They are really going to try to charge him with murder!*

I wagged my head. "Now Larry, how long have you known Uncle Jake? Do you think he's capable of committing murder? And you know that he has been caring for her for years."

"I don't want to believe it either, Rob, but it doesn't look good."

"I know he didn't intentionally kill her, and I will prove it, Larry. Please don't say anything to my uncle right now. It would send him over the edge."

"That's why I told you to come alone. I'll keep in touch. In the meantime, stay away from your uncle's house. We don't want you to be accused of tampering with evidence in an investigation."

"Oh, I wouldn't dream of doing that, Larry!"

"Just let me get back to you when I have more to go on."

On the way home I called Annette on my car phone. She was with a patient, so I left a message for her to ring me at home when she got free.

It was lunch time before I got her call. I had just taken some ham and cheese out of the fridge to make a sandwich.

"Hi, 'Nette. The Chief called me in. It seems that Aunt Hazel likely died of a morphine overdose."

"Oh no! You know Jake couldn't have killed her on purpose!"

"Of course not! But he has been giving her the shots for quite a while now and it doesn't set well with the police. They're continuing with their investigation."

Annette was silent for a moment; then said, "Well, all we can do is wait and see what comes of it. I'm glad you're his attorney."

I made my sandwich, got some corn chips and grabbed me a cold root beer to wash it down with. As I chomped on the sandwich I heard Uncle Jake stirring. I had finished eating by the time he came into the kitchen.

"Want some lunch, Uncle Jake?"

"I haven't had breakfast yet. I can get by with a bowl of raison bran, if you have some."

"No need to just 'get by!' I can fix you a couple of eggs and some toast. How do you like your eggs?"

"Now you *are* making me hungry! Just scramble 'em. Thanks a bunch."

I smiled and put a small frying pan on the stove.

"I know you don't want to think about it yet, but you and I are going to have to go to the funeral home and make some arrangements. Did they take her to Hamlar's?"

"Yeah. I knew that's where Papa and Mama were taken. I really appreciate your help. I can't believe she's really gone!"

I could hear a muffled choking. I know he cared about her, and wouldn't have done anything to hurt her, much less take her life.

For someone who usually wolfed his food down, Uncle Jake was awfully slow eating those two eggs. I felt like crying, but knew I needed to be strong for him.

We just sat around and chewed the fat all that afternoon. One incident he talked about was the time I insisted that he go with me to the Central Virginia Celtic Festival and Highland Games in Richmond. I had a cousin who played the bagpipes and he had convinced me to go a few times. It was enjoyable and Uncle Jake had really gotten a kick out of the music. It was before Aunt Hazel had gotten so bad off, but she had no desire to go with us.

He told me about buying a cassette tape of the Virginia Highland Pipes and Drums that my cousin, Aunt Liz's son, Ralph Gunn, was in and how much Hazel enjoyed it. The group was based in Vinton, just outside Roanoke, and traveled all over the state to play at the various Games.

Hazel loved the old ways and folk music. She just wasn't much on traveling away from home. I honestly don't think she set foot outside of Roanoke County in her whole life.

The entire afternoon was chocked full of Jake's reminiscences of good times that all led back to Hazel. I just let him talk. I knew it was good for him.

I still hadn't heard from Larry by the time Annette got home at 5:30.

I decided to order pizza delivery from Mellow Mushroom. We just needed time to be together as a family. Annette had had a tough day and we all just needed to chill a bit.

By 10:30 all three of us were ready to try to get a good night's rest. I told Jake we would go to the funeral home the next morning.

I wondered why I hadn't heard from Larry, but knew the call was bound to come the next day.

Chapter 5

My grandfather Blair had purchased a block of 20 burial plots at Fair View Cemetery back in 1953 when my grandmother passed. It was the oldest operational burial park in Roanoke County, being established in 1890. He had told all his children that these lots would be available to any of his descendants as long as there were vacant ones left. My grandfather was buried there in 1970 when he went to join his saintly wife.

Some family members had moved out of state to places like Michigan, Kentucky, North Carolina and Tennessee. Some of the ones who had died away from Virginia were buried where their wives' families were interred. There were still eight lots available, so we made arrangements to have Hazel buried there. Her nephews didn't object, seeing that Jake was footing the bill for the funeral.

After we made the arrangements, Jake was relieved that this was all taken care of, and wrote a check for the entire cost on the spot.

We drove into my driveway at 11:04 and my car phone was ringing. It was Larry.

"Let me call you back in a bit." I said softly.

I asked Uncle Jake to excuse me while I returned "a business call" in my little home office on our lower level.

"Hey Larry. I'm back with you. I was just pulling in the drive and Jake was with me. What's up?"

"Well, you're not going to like this, Rob. My officers went out yesterday afternoon and found a prescription bottle for 60 morphine pills filled four days before your aunt's death. It only had two pills left. It takes 16 of these a day to prepare for the injections. I called Dr. Smith and there were supposed to be two bottles and only one was found. We can't figure out what happened to the other bottle. We're going to have to bring your uncle back in for more questioning."

"Well, for heaven's sake, wait till after the funeral! It is Tuesday at 2:00 in the afternoon. At least give him till Wednesday."

"Okay, Rob. You got it. I'll see you at the funeral."

The next few days I tried to be as level headed as I could. Uncle Jake insisted that I go back to work on Monday. He asked if he could stay with us until after the funeral. I told him that I wouldn't have it any other way.

At my office everyone was beyond nice to me and told me how very sorry they were about my aunt's death. I knew that Allen and his wife, Alberta, as well as my secretary, Susan McKay, and her fiancé, George Baker, would be at the funeral. In fact, we all agreed to close the office the entire next day. Susan bought a wreath for the door.

"Let not your heart be troubled, ye have believed in God, believe also in me. In my father's house are many mansions. If it were not so I would have told you. I go to prepare a place for you. And if I go and prepare a place for you, I will come again, and receive you unto myself, that where I am, there ye may be also."

It was Mark Price doing the eulogy. I didn't know why he was using the King James Bible. Her family must have gotten hold of him. In church he always read from the Revised Standard

Version. Mark was the pastor of the First Presbyterian Church. Our families had been friends since before he was born. Jake was pleased, though he had never darkened the door of a church, that I knew of. I knew he had gotten good raising, though, by Christian parents.

Two of Aunt Hazel's nephews and my son, Jonathan, who came in from North Carolina, as well as my brother Bill's three sons served as pallbearers. At the grave my daughter, Louisa, laid the first flower on the casket.

"Ashes to ashes and dust to dust. The Lord giveth and the Lord taketh away. Blessed be the name of the Lord."

When we got home our children all came to the house. In spite of the circumstances, it was good to have our kids all home again, even for just a day or two.

We all went out to dinner that night at Red Lobster on Franklin Road. That was a restaurant we could all agree on.

I got their sampler plate, and I knew that Annette would go for the lobster tail. "Just enough," she always said. "Don't need a whole lobster!"

We had four bedrooms and Uncle Jake was in one, so we only had two more. Louisa could have gone home, but wanted to stay in her old room for the nostalgia.

Robert Jr., who lived in Arlington, volunteered to stay at Howard Johnson's. He liked their breakfast anyway, he said.

But his liking their breakfast didn't hold water. He came back the next morning and joined the rest of us for breakfast before they all left.

Our large split-level home seemed empty again once we said our goodbyes.

They hadn't been gone but about ten minutes when the phone rang. I held my breath.

Chapter 6

"Good morning, Larry."

"I need to talk to Jake. Put him on the phone."

"Don't be too harsh with him!"

"Just let me talk to him!"

He was still at the kitchen table.

"Uncle Jake, I shouted from the living room. "Chief Watts wants to holler at you a minute." *Oops, that came out wrong!*

"Good morning, Chief. What can I do ya for?"

"Something has come up that I need to ask you about. Can you please come by the station as soon as possible?"

"Well, Rob is going to take me home after lunch. I guess he wouldn't mind bringing me by there on the way."

"Sounds good. See you this afternoon."

"What do you suppose they want this time? I told him everything I know the other morning."

"Oh, you know how these things are, Uncle Jake. They drag out these blamed investigations. It gives 'em something to do to spend our tax dollars. We just have to go by and see what he says."

At lunch Uncle Jake seemed pensive and quiet. I just decided not to ask any questions or volunteer any information. It would all hit the fan soon enough.

Larry looked up from his desk, laid his cigarette in the ash tray and took his reading glasses off as we walked in.

"Sit down gentlemen! I was at the funeral yesterday, but had to leave before I had a chance to speak to either of you. You know how this damn job is. I got a buzz on my pager and had to call in."

I let out a deep breath.

"Yeah, I saw you, Larry. Thanks for coming."

"Jake, the coroner, Dr. Patel, did an autopsy at my request to determine the cause of death. He said it was almost certainly a morphine overdose. It's going to take about four months to get the lab results back.

"I sent two of my best officers out to your house and they found a bottle of morphine pills that was almost empty. That wasn't the problem. Doc Smith, your wife's physician, says that there should have been two bottles. One should have been full. We couldn't find the other bottle anywhere! What did you do with it?"

Uncle Jake's mouth flew open and a frown gripped his brow. It took him several seconds to answer.

"Ole Doc Smith is flat out wrong! We only get one bottle of 60 pills at a time! It takes 16 pills a day, so they go awful' fast. I'm always running to the drug store to get more. But you know with something like morphine they won't let you have 120 pills at a time!"

"The doc said he gave you a bottle the last time you were at his office and then you went and took the prescription to the drug store that same day!"

"I don't remember him giving me any pills! If he did, they may have dropped out of the car somewhere we stopped before we got to our house. I remember getting home and having to go back out to get the pills."

"Well, Jake, since you obviously don't have anyone to back up your story, I'm gonna to have to arrest you on suspicion of the murder of your wife."

Jake broke down crying. Two uniforms came in and cuffed my dear uncle and led him out.

"I want him released in my custody!" I snapped.

"That'll have to wait till he goes before Judge Parker!"

"We'll just see about that! Judge Parker is a personal friend of mine, you know!"

And off I went to the courthouse to wait for the session to break.

Chapter 7

It was 5:00 o'clock before I got to speak with the judge. I knew he could tell I wanted to see him, because he glanced back at me several times and I gave him a hand up at least twice.

My mind had been wandering to the two cases I had on the next criminal docket and the fact that I would have to take more time to prepare for them. One was a murder case of a man who allegedly robbed a convenience store and shot the clerk; another was assault with a deadly weapon—a tire iron at a garage. My world couldn't come to an end because my uncle was being charged with suspicion of murder.

Judge Parker motioned for me to follow him into his chambers when he saw me marching toward him.

"What is it that would make you sit all afternoon in my court when your time goes for big bucks, Rob?"

With a sour look, I stared at him and did my best to explain the situation.

"Hank, My uncle Jake is being held on suspicion of murdering his wife. First of all, you know he isn't capable of such a thing; there's not a cruel bone in his body! There has to be a logical explanation for what happened. Secondly, you know he isn't a flight risk. Where would he go? He has one of the most valuable homes and estates in Roanoke. I need you to let him be released on his own recognizance until they have enough to make a real charge. I will keep him at my house."

"I heard about your aunt's death and I am terribly sorry, Rob. What evidence does Larry have on him?"

"Her death was allegedly caused by an overdose of morphine and Uncle Jake gives her the shots. They sent for a toxicology report to confirm it. They can't find a bottle of pills that her doctor says she had. But you know that he couldn't kill her! Not intentionally, anyway! I need some time to find out the facts. And Uncle Jake doesn't need to be setting in jail with real criminals."

"I'll have to call the Chief and clear this."

"Hey, Larry, Rob Blair is here in my chambers and is asking for his uncle to be released on his own recognizance in his custody. What's your take on that?"

"Sorry, Hank, no can do. I just spoke with the D.A. and she assures me that she has enough to make the charge stick without the lab report. The photos taken at the hospital of Hazel, which Ms. Brown examined, show that Hazel's lips and fingertips had turned blue. A sure sign of overdose. I'm surprised Patel failed to mention that.

"Given the circumstances, I will consider his release only with sufficient bail money. But don't make it easy on them. They can afford it."

"Thanks Chief. Copy that, as you boys say."

"Well, Rob, the news isn't good. The D.A. is making a charge of murder because of sufficient evidence. They have more than you have been told about. He's your uncle and I trust you implicitly, however, I'm going to grant bail in the amount of $50,000."

$50,000? Why are you doing this, Hank? That's outlandish!"

"Think, Rob, think! This is going to get out and if I set low bail people would say that he was given special preference because he's your uncle."

I ducked my head. "I see what you mean. I can't think straight right now. I'll put it up myself."

I got a signed statement of bail from the judge and drove back to the jail.

Uncle Jake bear hugged me and held on like it was the end of the world and I was his only hope of salvation.

"You know that until he goes to trial," Larry said, "he will have to stay with you."

"Of course! That's a given. I'm going to get to the bottom of this!"

Chapter 8

The main front page headline the next morning, Thursday, July 4th had nothing to do with celebrating the anniversary of our nation's independence:

Jacob Blair Arrested on Murder Charge

The *Roanoke Gazette* was never known for telling decent things about people. The more juicy the scoop, the better.

As the smoky steam from my coffee arose before my eyes, I read the entire cruel article. My heart skipped a beat. It emphasized the fact that Jake was the uncle of one of the most celebrated attorneys in town and that bail had been arranged without a bail hearing. They weren't painting me like Perry Mason. More like Tom Hagen in *The Godfather*.

Of course they made it seem like Jake was guilty until proven innocent.

I tried to keep Uncle Jake from getting his hands on the paper, but he had seen the glaring headline over my shoulder as he entered the kitchen. I knew he would find out about it before long anyway. Hiding things never works in the long run.

He sat down next to me and I just pushed the newspaper in his direction.

"You know how that bunch down at the *Gazette* is, Uncle Jake. Don't pay any attention to them. We do need to talk, though. This will be going before the Grand Jury before long and we have to be ready."

Jake just gazed up at me with a pitiful puppy look on his face like he didn't know what to say. I decided I would give him a little time to collect his thoughts. It would be a little while before we had to face the music.

Annette and I both went on to work. I just told Jake not to leave the house because I was responsible for him and we couldn't take any chances on someone attacking him. People get crazy when they believe the worst about someone.

He smiled and said he understood.

That day at the office I called Larry and got brought up to speed on the evidence.

I told Susan to only put through calls to me from Annette, Jake or one of my clients. I went to work on preparation for the Johnson case, the guy who flatly denied shooting the store clerk. He admitted to the robbery, but said that another man came in, saw him holding a gun on the clerk and opened fire at him, inadvertently hitting the clerk. When that happened, according to Johnson, the stranger bolted. Johnson had ditched his gun in the Roanoke River and we couldn't prove that the fatal shot didn't come from his gun. It was up to me to create reasonable doubt in the mind of the jurors.

In mid afternoon a call came in from someone claiming to be Johnson's brother in order to get through to me.

"Blair, I'm a cousin of your aunt on her mother's side. I'm going to see that that murdering uncle of yours pays for what he did one way or the other!"

"What is your name, sir? Where are you calling from?"

The thunderous sound of the receiver being slammed down echoed throughout my head. I sure wasn't going to tell Uncle Jake about this call. I quickly pushed the speed dial for Larry's private line.

"Larry, we may have a problem. I just got a call threatening my uncle. What can you do?"

"Now you know damn well that there is nothing I can do! I couldn't even do anything if I knew who it was. The best thing I can tell you at this point is that if he calls again—it was a man, right?"

"Yes, a man with a gruff-sounding voice."

"I can put a tap on your phone and if he calls again, have your secretary call us and keep him on the line as long as you can. We will also record it. We can try to trace the call. Then we can have something to go on if he says anything against the law."

I emitted a long sigh. "Okay, go ahead and set up the tap. My home phone is unlisted, so I don't think he can call me there."

At least I had been able to formulate a line of defense for Johnson before this nerve-wracking call came in. I would have to keep close tabs on my uncle.

That night I told him that the newspaper had stirred up a hornet's nest and I wanted him to let me know if anything strange happened when we weren't home.

"I think you're just gettin' carried away over nothing, Robbie. Don't worry about me; I'll be fine as frog's hair."

"Nevertheless, it's always better to be safe than sorry."

Jake smiled and nodded. I think he just didn't want to be a burden.

Chapter 9

Friday night we watched "The Quiet Man" for the umpteenth time. I owned the VHS. It was one of those movies that I never tired of. It had always been my favorite John Wayne flick because it was unique for him; neither a western nor a war movie. He co-starred with Maureen O'Hara, a great on-screen match for him, as an Irishman who had come home from America to buy the family's homestead.

We all just took it in and tried to relax as much as possible.

Saturday morning the three of us all slept in till about 9:30. Some people thought that was the normal time to get up and laughed when I told them we "slept in" till 9:30. Then Annette fixed us a big breakfast of eggs, sausage, and gravy and biscuits with fruit, coffee and orange juice.

After breakfast, while Annette cleaned up the kitchen, I took Uncle Jake into the den for a serious powwow. It was time.

44

"Uncle Jake, please start at the beginning. What else should I know about Aunt Hazel? Do you think she could have been taking morphine shots on her own when you were out?"

"I wouldn't think so. But remember; she was in awful pain and was losing her will to live."

"What defense do you think we should use?"

"Just don't change anything I told them. Say that it is my contention that I didn't have another bottle of pills."

"But, Uncle Jake! That doesn't change the fact that she died of an overdose of morphine.

"You could add that she was losing her will to live and could have had someone help her take additional morphine when I wasn't home—that is if there were more pills. I was out working a lot of the time. Sometimes I had to go into town for groceries and supplies."

I thought for a minute and said, "Okay. I'll do that. But when it goes before the grand jury we need a reason for them to reject the case."

*****

On Monday morning I got another call from the mysterious cousin. I signaled Susan to call Larry.

"Robert Blair, may I help you?"

"Yes, nigger lover, they tell me that not only are you defending that SOB uncle of yours, you're also representing that murdering nigger, Johnson! I'm not coming after Johnson right now, first things first. But I want you to drop your uncle, because he killed my cousin! I have a lot of friends who can see to it that he never lives to see the light of day again after he goes back into the system."

"Just what do you want me to do? How would it look if I refused to defend my own uncle?"

"I don't know, and I don't give a rat's ass. How would it look if you ended up dead? Your uncle isn't gonna live very long anyhow."

"If you would just tell me who you are and where I can meet you, I will be glad to talk to you about how we need to go about this."

"No thanks, jerk. You're just trying to trick me. Obviously you want to trace this call. I'll be in touch later."

"Susan, call the police station and see if they got the call traced!"

Just about that time the phone rang again.

"Sorry, Rob. We lacked five seconds having enough time. But I know who it was; I know his voice. And you aren't going to like it."

"Who?"

"Jesse Henshaw. The Grand Dragon of the Ku Klux Klan for Southwest Virginia. He is a first cousin to Hazel."

"How do we find him?"

"You and I probably couldn't. But I have an undercover officer who has a CI with under-ground connections. It'll be risky, but I think we can locate his meeting place and find out when their next gathering is."

"Well, for heaven sake, get on it right away!"

Chapter 10

That night I had a horrifying nightmare! It was 1954 and I was playing with my little black friend, Jody Lusk. I was taught to be colorblind. "All people are God's creation," my mother had told me.

In my dream, Jody and I were wrestling playfully and giggling. We were both ten years old. Junior Danner, the school bully, came up and knocked me off of Jody and beat me within an inch of my life!

"We don't need sissies like you around playing with niggers! Why, I think you're part darky yourself!"

Junior's buddy, Andy "Ace" Sewell started roaring with laughter.

I looked around and we were the only four people on the school playground. I yelled for help and no one came. Then Junior picked Jody and me up and banged our heads together. I woke up in a cold sweat, screaming. Annette pulled me to her shoulder and kissed me gently on my cheek.

"It was just a bad dream, Honey. Everything's alright. Go back to sleep."

The dream made no sense, anyway. Our school was segregated. The only times I had gotten to play with Jody had been when my dad took me along when he was visiting Jody's grandfather, Will Boden. Dad and Mr. Boden had gotten to be good friends because of the cattle business. Dad bought suckling calves from him in the fall because he wasn't able to winter them on his small farm.

I was sure glad it was the weekend! In the morning when we awakened, I was determined to attend church.

"Uncle Jake, I'm afraid I must insist on your going to church with us this morning. I need to tell you now that someone is threatening us because of your situation and we will have to make sure that you are either with us, or we have a guard on the house while we're away."

Uncle Jake looked startled.

"Who on earth would threaten us?"

"Do you know Aunt Hazel's cousin, Jesse Henshaw?"

"Well, not personally, but I know he's not the type of fella you would want to trust your daughter with."

"That's putting it mildly, Uncle Jake. He is the Grand Dragon of the Ku Klux Klan!"

"Is that bunch of heathen still operating?"

"I'm afraid so. They don't want people to think they are, but they are. And he already didn't like me because I defend blacks. But he's out to get you and me both, apparently."

"I'm so sorry that I've put you in the middle of this mess, Robbie."

"You can't help it, Uncle Jake. We just have to get through it. And get through it we will!"

"Okey dokey! I'll go to church with you folks this morning."

I took Uncle Jake by his house to pick up a few clothes and get ready for church.

That morning Mark's sermon was on John 13:34:

"I give you a new commandment, that you love one another. Just as I have loved you, you also should love one another."

It was hard to think about loving this scoundrel, Henshaw, *but, he isn't one of us*, I reasoned. I was still glad Mark didn't preach on "an eye for an eye and a tooth for a tooth!"

Chapter 11

The next few days were quiet ones. Almost too quiet. I had asked Larry for a plain white wrapper to be parked near my house from 8:00 to 6:00 each week day until things came to a head or settled down. I was surprised, but he didn't give me any lip about it. Hopefully it wouldn't be for long.

That Thursday, Judge Parker set Wednesday July 31st as the date for the Grand Jury to convene and the selection process began that following Monday.

I surmised that our "friend" was waiting until the decision was made about this case before taking further action or making more threats.

Things at home were as normal as could be expected and only once was anything suspected to be out of the ordinary. The officer found out that it was only a teenager sneaking into the house next door to meet his girl friend.

Finally the date arrived and the Grand Jury all showed up. It took them less than an hour to decide that there was enough evidence to take Uncle Jake to trial.

Trial date was set for Monday October 21st at 8:00 AM.

Since Jake was out on bail and all seemed to be in order, the bail held up. Now I had to go to work.

I needed a plan, and I was going to drill Uncle Jake again.

Late one Tuesday evening in mid-August, he and I were setting on the patio in the back of the house. The moon was in the waxing crescent and a pale circle was formed around it. Dark clouds were gathering, so I knew that a summer shower was on the way.

"All the evidence is circumstantial, and that goes in our favor. I still can't help but feel that there is something you aren't telling me. Uncle Jake, I am more than your nephew, I'm your lawyer. Everything you tell me goes under client confidentiality. Nothing you say will go any further. And you know I love you."

Uncle Jake was not answering. Suddenly I heard a sound of glass shattering and Annette's shrill scream coming from inside the house! In addition there was the chilling squeal of Molly, our calico cat, as she dashed for one of her favorite hiding places in our bedroom closet. I could almost visualize her short multi-colored hair standing straight on end as the harrowing episode unfolded.

I flew as fast as my short legs would carry me in the back door and saw a flaming glass bottle catching the living room carpet on fire. Luckily, I knew without giving it a thought where the fire extinguisher was hanging in the hall closet and had its white fizzy contents beamed on the Molotov cocktail which threatened to destroy my home!

That monster, Henshaw, had found out where I lived and now we were on the top of his list to eliminate!

I got on the horn and called Larry at home.

"You're not going to believe what happened!"

"You won the lottery?"

"Don't you get smart with me, Larry! We just had a Molotov cocktail thrown through our front window!"

I could almost see the look on Larry's face.

"Oh my God, Rob! Well, I don't know what to tell you at the minute, but I do have some good news for you. Our CI found out when the Klan is meeting next and where. They're rallying at the Old Salem Schoolhouse this Saturday night. Just be on guard, and I'll have a patrol car drive by your house every hour at night. I am already tying up an officer there ten hours a day! That's costing the city some real dough."

"Well, what are you doing about that meeting?"

"We're sending out the vice squad to arrest Henshaw. We have his voice recorded from that call threatening you, and don't touch that bottle. I hope we can get some prints off of it."

"I'm sure he will lawyer up. We have to get Jake's trial underway. I'm working on his defense."

Uncle Jake was shaking like the last maple leaf on a tree in a windstorm when he came back in. I hadn't even thought a lot about how this was affecting Annette. My poor wife! She had a hard enough time dealing with some of her difficult patients. She surely didn't need this traumatic drama on top of that.

I reached over and took Annette in my arms and hugged her tightly.

"Do you feel like you need to go to your mother's until this is settled, Honey?"

Before she could answer, Jake spoke up.

"This isn't her fault. It's all mine. I have to talk to you, Rob. Annette doesn't need to go anywhere."

Chapter 12

Jake insisted on heading back out on the patio. The clouds had thickened, the wind had picked up to what must have been forty mile an hour gusts and lightning was flashing through the firmament to our west.

"Are you sure being out here is a good idea, Uncle Jake?"

"This won't take long, son. Tomorrow I want you to take me back to the jail where I can be placed in protective custody. I want it to be published in the local rag that that is what happened so they will leave you alone. They want me. They are afraid you will win the case and get me off."

"Say what?"

Jake started over with his story and told me a strikingly different one. Part of it included the fact that that night he and Aunt Hazel offered up a sincere prayer of surrender and dedication. He apologized for misleading me earlier, but admitted to increasing her doses at her insistence because her pain had grown to be so excruciating. He had never meant to kill her. I finally understood, and I felt sorry for my poor uncle. He was not guilty of murder.

Suddenly I recalled exactly what I had seen that night and a shiver ran down my spine like I had been hit by one of those lightning bolts we had seen in the west! But I kept silent.

We had to rush back into the house because the storm had gotten fierce fast and we were getting drenched.

The next morning I did exactly as he had asked. I hated to see him sit in a cold, hard jail cell, but it was less than two months till the trial, and even though Henshaw would be in jail for a minute, I knew we hadn't heard the end of this by a long shot. His lawyer would have him out before I could say Jack Robinson, and we would have hell to pay for detaining him. At least we had a case against him and could take him to trial when the time was right.

Annette called the glass company to replace our picture window.

The bottle was taken in to the local lab, and just as I suspected, there were no clear prints on it.

That Saturday night Larry's squad pulled off their raid on the Klan meeting without a hitch. The old white school building was surrounded and Henshaw was arrested as planned. No one else was taken in, because he was the only one they had any evidence on.

I could have almost predicted to the minute what ensued. Henshaw clammed up and neither admitted nor denied anything the cops said. He was out in two shakes of a lamb's tail.

But Jake was still in, and I was glad they couldn't go after him.

The cops circled by our house regularly as Larry had promised. One thing I could count on was the Chief's word.

There were no more attacks on my home, so I was still a bit puzzled as where this ogre was going with this, and his motive.

My defense was clear. It wasn't what I had hoped for, but at least it was a decent one. One that would paint my uncle as a good, moral man and clear him of the charge against him.

In the weeks leading up to the trial I had to get my mind on my other primary client. I went ahead and tried the Johnson case and came out smelling like a rose.

I was able to locate the other man who had entered the store and shot the clerk by the testimony of a witness who had actually seen him leave—an elderly woman who had been shopping across the street and taking her groceries to her car. It was really last minute. I was already creating reasonable doubt, but when I was actually able to produce the guilty party, I felt like celebrating.

My other case wasn't looking as good and I got a continuance because of my preparations for Uncle Jake's trial.

That night there was already a noisy throng gathering downtown; both those supporting Uncle Jake and those wanting to see him fried.

All of the three major national television networks had the crews of their morning shows checked in to the Heart of Roanoke Hotel.

I saw it all on the 11:00 news and my anxiety level went through the roof.

On the morning Jake's trial was to be held, however, I received a dreadful call from Larry.

Chapter 13

"**R**ob, I am terribly sorry to have to be the bearer of such bad news, but we found your uncle dead in his cell this morning. I'm having the coroner determine the cause of his death."

My heart dropped like a brick off the observatory on the 102nd floor of the Empire State Building. I gasped so loudly that someone must have been able to hear me a block away and started choking up.

"Oh, God, no! No! No! Was anyone else in the cell with him?"

"There was not."

"Who went in there last night?"

"Just the custodian who takes him his meals."

"Did you see any evidence of foul play? Suffocation or strangling?"

"Nothing, Rob."

"Well, I'm on my way over now! Is Dr. Patel there?"

"He is on his way, too. He should be here any minute."

When I reached the jail I saw Patel's car in the lot. My mind was racing. *Who could have done this? Why?*

Patel's face was solemn. He was bending over the stiff body of my dear uncle.

"What was the time of death, Dr. Patel?" I asked.

"Judging from the state of rigor mortis, I would say around 10:00 last night."

"Can you tell the cause of death yet?"

"It was certainly natural causes. From looking at his charts and seeing his condition and the medications he was taking, I am ruling that death was caused by a heart attack."

This was just a little too convenient! A fatal heart attack the night before he was to go to trial? Jake had told me they were after him. But *why? Who?*

Not only would I have to prove that he was killed; I had to prove by whom and for what

63

purpose. This head-scratching mystery was deepening all the time.

I wasn't born yesterday, and my wife was a doctor. I would get a second opinion. But what reason would Patel have to mask a murder?

I thought I had better play it super cool.

"I'll call the funeral home," I said, as I walked to the front desk. "May I use your phone?"

I went on home, knowing that Jim at Hamlar's Funeral Home would be there soon and there was no more damage that anyone could do to his body. I had told him not to begin the embalming process until Annette had taken the body to the hospital and had an autopsy performed. From the phone in my car, I called Annette and she was as nervous as a cat in a room full of rocking chairs. I asked her to tell her assistant that she had an emergency and to call her patients to reset her appointments for the rest of the morning. She must get by the funeral home within the next hour to remove Jake's body to the hospital for an autopsy.

Within three hours, Annette buzzed me at the office. I had briefly told the others what had happened and asked for time alone.

"Short answer, Uncle Jake was given a drug in his food or drink which made it appear that he had a myocardial infarction. The pathologist also ran a blood test. We have to keep this to ourselves until we can conduct a full investigation."

That I knew. But now I wondered who I could trust.

Chapter 14

We had the damning results of the autopsy and blood test in hand and that would stand up in court when we had this pile of ropes untangled.

I drove by Hamlar's and sat down with Jim to plan the arrangements for Jake's funeral.

That Saturday I went into my little office at home after a long breakfast and frank chat with Annette about the predicament we were in. I had to figure out why someone wanted Uncle Jake dead so I could get to the bottom of this dastardly plot.

In the Commonwealth of Virginia, when someone died intestate all real estate and personal property passed from a deceased spouse to the living one at death; then to the living brothers and sisters of the remaining spouse at his or her passing. If a brother or sister had passed away, his or her portion would go to the living heirs. Very simple. How well I remembered their both telling me that they didn't need wills because the laws would do exactly what they wanted done without them. Well... Jake had told me that and Hazel had said, "Yeah."

Since there were no children involved, I really couldn't argue with that logic, though I told them it was highly unusual to have no wills when there was so high a property value.

Now we had a valuable estate which would pass to Uncle Jake's heirs, including my father.

So the property would not go to her family anyway. Even if it would, why would a cousin of his deceased wife be interested in this? He wouldn't have been an heir either way.

I sucked in a big puff of air and slowly let it out.

The funeral was gloomy and not that many attended it. Naturally he was buried next to Hazel. I was glad that Jake and I had picked out a classy stone that would include the two of them there in the Blair section of Fair View. The autumn leaves were turning so many brilliant hues. Poplars dressed in their bright golden yellows, maples in crimson and orange, and white oaks blanching to a pale blonde-brown.

I tried so desperately to get my wits about me and dwell on the beauty of nature rather than the ugliness of human debauchery.

Ironically, the next day after Uncle Jake's funeral the positive toxicology report came back. The news media was not informed, nor would they have been interested. There was no longer a story for them to exploit.

It was four weeks later, on Tuesday, November 24th, when I received a subpoena from the attorneys for Ray Blair, and Hazel's other nephews and nieces, which Susan had scanned and briefed me on, demanding that the estate of Jake and Hazel Blair be turned over to them.

What the heck? Turned over to them?

I opened up the subpoena and read their contention after the acknowledgement of the marriage and joint ownership of the property:

Hazel F. Blair died intestate on June 26, 1991. Plaintiffs aver that Jacob Richard Blair her husband, was the "slayer" as defined in Section 66-401 of the Code of Virginia, 1950. As amended.

On October 17, 1991, Jacob Richard Blair, died intestate.

Plaintiffs are the legal heirs of Hazel F. Blair as defined by Title 64.1 of the Code of Virginia. 1950, as amended, and would be entitled under Title 64.1 to that share of this decedent's property that would have passed to the "slayer".

THEREFORE, Plaintiffs move this honorable Court for a severance of the interest of the decedent, Jacob Richard Blair, with respect to that property held as Tenants by the Entirety and that this Court Order that interest to be so distributed as provided by law.

So this was their little game, huh? And they couldn't have played this card if my uncle had lived and I had gotten him off. Not even knowing my line of defense, they ran scared and jumped from the frying pan into the fire.

Uh-huh! Their real estate alone was worth in excess of $2,000,000, even at that time. And they both had valuable antiques, to boot.

Well, we would just see about this! They're playing against the wrong cardsharp!

Chapter 15

I knew that this had to be a conspiracy. Even a blind man could have seen that. Jesse Henshaw had nothing to gain unless by arrangement with Ray Blair, et al. And what was up with Patel? Why had he been so quick to label Jake's cause of death as a heart attack with no autopsy? Two and two still didn't total up to five. I didn't need my doctorate to figure that one out.

I called Larry and asked for his CI to give me a call. I didn't want to meet him or know his name. I wasn't about to jeopardize his position.

About 3:35 that afternoon my phone rang. I asked him if Ray, Sam or John Blair had been at that Ku Klux Klan meeting. He told me that Ray was the only one of them that he knew; but, yes, he was there.

Bingo! Pay dirt! But I dared not move too fast.

I thanked him and told him that he had been very helpful.

Now for more digging.

Ray had a listed home phone. He worked for a lumber mill as a supervisor, so I knew I couldn't track him there. I called Larry right before 5:00 and requested a tap on his line based on this new information.

I told Larry about the autopsy, the subpoena and my believed connection of Hazel's nephews to the plot to kill Uncle Jake. He acted very concerned and asked me to be careful, but readily agreed to tap Ray's phone for me.

He told me that he would send Joe Jenks by my house that night. He was a detective, he explained, that helped him out on special assignments. He had been one of the officers that had guarded my house while Jake was staying there.

We had just finished a delicious fried chicken dinner when the doorbell chimed.

"Joe, good to meet you," I said, reaching for his hand.

Joe was immaculately dressed with not a hair out of place.

"This is my wife, Annette; she's a general practitioner here in Roanoke. Her office is over near General Hospital."

"Good to meet you, ma'am!" Joe tipped the hard brim of his round uniform hat.

"The pleasure is all mine, Detective! Come on in. Would you like a cup of decaf coffee? I just made a fresh pot. We enjoy it after dinner."

"Don't mind if I do. I would even take some high octane about now since I'm on duty!'

They both laughed and Annette brought us all a cup in her best china.

"Larry tells me that you're investigating your uncle's alleged murder. What makes you think he was murdered? Word was that he died of natural causes. Heart attack, wasn't it?"

"That's what we thought at first. But there were some circumstances that made me doubt Dr. Patel's diagnosis, so I had Annette get an autopsy done by a forensic pathologist at the hospital."

Joe frowned. "Well, you have to be careful with accusing people of something unless you have conclusive proof. I've known Anand Patel since right after he came to Roanoke and I've always found him to be above board. I'm sure if he was wrong it was an honest mistake."

"I was going to ask you your opinion of him, but I guess you've already given me that."

"Yes, sir!" Joe smiled and took a long sip of his coffee. "Is there anything else you need to know?"

"Not right now. Thanks. I guess I can look in other directions. You have a nice evening, Joe."

I wanted to let him know that there was really no sense in his staying any longer.

There was just something a bit off-plum about Mr. "Too Pretty". The way he reacted to my concerns showed me that I would get no sympathy out of him. And he admitted to being friends with Dr. Patel. If Larry had a bad apple in his department I would have to be even more cautious.

Chapter 16

After giving the matter my deepest consideration, I made the decision to go outside the Roanoke area to get professional help. I had a Richmond phonebook at my office, so I checked the yellow pages for private eyes. Cost was not a problem. We had considerable investments and a comfortable amount in savings. Of course I told Annette what I was planning to do.

One catchy ad, in particular, caught my attention:

"Private investigator Barry Black, satisfaction guaranteed or your money back."

Now that was a new one! And I liked the old boy's confidence. I set an appointment with his secretary to see him on Monday December 9th at 9:30. I didn't tell anyone what I was doing.

It was a cool day with drizzle and frequent bursts of wind that morning as I headed up I-81 toward East I-64. It felt like it could turn to snow, but luckily the temperature was forecast to rise slightly that morning. What would normally be less than a three hour drive on a clear mid-day run took me four hours and ten minutes because of weather and traffic. Luckily I planned for it and got to Black's office by 9:15.

I guess he had to let me know that he was important, because he kept me waiting till almost 9:45.

At first glance I felt more like Perry Mason, because I had found my Paul Drake! He was tall and handsome with sandy-blond hair, blue eyes and a winning smile.

"Good morning, Mr. Blair. Sorry for the delay, I was on the phone with a client. Come on into my office."

I couldn't let on that I was jealous of his looks. I had red hair and freckles and was 5' 9".

"Mr. Black, I want to cut to the chase. I know your time is valuable, as is mine. I have a problem telling who in Roanoke is wearing white hats and who has on the black ones.

My aunt by marriage died of a morphine overdose and her side of the family is trying to say that my uncle was the slayer and couldn't inherit their estate. In the meantime, apparently because they were afraid I might get him off in court, somebody slipped a dangerous drug into his food in jail, where he had chosen to be for self-protection. I am certain that the Ku Klux Klan is involved because one of her cousins is the Grand Dragon and was threatening us.

Aunt Hazel's nephews are also involved, primarily one named Ray. He's apparently mixed up with the Klan also. Oh, by the way, they are distant cousins of our family. It's Ray Blair. He works for Berring and Harper Lumber Company in Vinton. I'm having his phone tapped.

"To top it all off, I have reason to believe that the coroner and a police detective named Joe Jenks are also involved in this. I really don't have a clue why these folks would get mixed up in something like this, but the Police Chief is a friend of mine and I'm sure he isn't going to believe that one of his own is taking part in a conspiracy against my family. He told me that he trusts Jenks completely."

"You do have quite a tangled web, don't you Mr. Blair?"

"Yes, and please call me Rob. All my friends do, and if we're going to be working together, I certainly hope we will be friends."

Black smiled. "And you need to call me Barry. Based on what you have told me I think I need to put a loose tail on the coroner. What's his name?"

"Dr. Anand Patel. He came to Roanoke from here in Richmond."

"I'll do some checking on him and send one of my men over to follow him after work each day. Getting what I need to know shouldn't be too difficult since he used to practice in Richmond. But we can't do anything to arouse suspicion."

I went back to Aunt Hazel's death and gave Barry a complete rundown on everything that had happened. I told him about the Molotov cocktail that had landed in our living room, Henshaw's arrest and release, and gave him everybody's name and phone number—the ones I had, that I believed were in any way involved with this mystery.

Barry told me that he would start with Patel and get back to me as soon as he had anything useful. He said that it might be slow, but he would get to the bottom of things.

I felt much better as I drove home that day. After I got back to Roanoke, I stopped for lunch at Shoney's and went on to my law office, arriving at 1:20.

I had barely opened the door when Susan yelled out, "You had a call from some guy named Black. He says it's important."

Chapter 17

"**H**ey Barry! I wasn't expecting to hear from you this quick!"

"Yeah, well, I wasn't expecting to have anything this soon either. It's about Patel, of course. He left Richmond under a shadow. The hospital he worked for suspected him of assisting in a patient suicide. They couldn't prove it, but they had reason to believe that he was paid well by a deposit from the lady's estate. The thing was, she wasn't terminally ill; just emotionally disturbed. She was almost 85 years old. Her husband had died of prostate cancer. She felt like she had nothing to live for.

"This leads me to believe that Patel is capable of taking someone's life for money. At least it's fuel to feed the fire when we need it."

"Thanks, Barry. I hope you have something else within the next few days."

That Thursday I got a plea on the mechanic. He agreed to cop for manslaughter and serve five years on probation including time already served. I was just glad it was over.

I wasn't hearing anything from Larry, so I decided to give him a call on Friday. He told me that he had been tied up with an arson case regarding a low-rent apartment building. The property owner had raised everyone's rent and refused to fix the plumbing. One of the irate tenants had moved his meager belongings out to a storage unit and set the building on fire. He had eluded the police and had now been spotted in Charlottesville. Larry was working with their department to try to apprehend him.

Out of sight, out of mind on my case.

I was mighty glad I had hired Barry.

Annette and I had talked about going away that weekend, but the weather was too cold to even think about it. I needed to do some Christmas shopping anyway, so I spent the day Saturday at the mall looking for toys for my grandchildren and clothes for Annette. She looked like a queen in anything she wore, but there were still styles to consider and I was no expert in that field.

I could have gone to Liz's boutique, but I didn't even want her to know what I was getting Annette. There was a clerk I trusted at Macy's and I knew that she was up to date on what was chic because she always looked like she stepped out of a fashion magazine.

Annette consistently beat me with completing her holiday shopping, as she started every year in October. But I was pretty sure I got better deals by waiting till closer to Christmas. I still avoided Black Friday. I wasn't going to be trampled by some desperate parent wanting a steal on a limited special of the latest video game.

When I got home, I found a note from my lady saying that she had decided to take the day with our daughter and would bring home our dinner from Red Lobster. Oh yeah! I really wished Louisa would come over more often, but I would see her and her fiancé when I could. Of course she was tied up in him. I thought she was too young to be engaged. Christmas would be there soon. Yeah, dinner from Red Lobster sounded pretty darn good to me.

Sunday morning it came a heavy, wet snow and we stayed home and watched *It's a Wonderful Life*. We both enjoy old movies even to this day.

Annette and I lounged all day in our PJs and snuggled that night making beautiful love together. Since this disastrous turn of events had come upon us, this hadn't happened often enough.

"In times like these we need each other more than ever, 'Nette, Baby." I said as I lay close to her shapely form. Now that I have Barry Black on the job, I hope the tide will start to turn."

"I sure hope so, Honey, I sure hope so."

Chapter 18

I was getting new potential clients calling, but I wasn't accepting them all. I had to allow time for our case and for the holidays with our family.

It was just two days before the 'jolly old elf' was to arrive, on a Monday morning, when I got my next phone call from Barry.

"I hate to contact you this close to Christmas, Rob, but this couldn't wait. Last night the 'good doctor' met with Ray Blair at a little out-of-the-way restaurant. My man couldn't get too close, for obvious reasons, but Ray had a small piece of what appeared to be ore in his hand showing it to Patel. My man heard Ray say the word "titanium." Then he heard Patel say, "I just had to see it for myself.""

"My God! Do you know what this means?"

"Sure I do. That ore supposedly came from your uncle's farm!"

Now it was beginning to fit into place.

"Wait a minute," I said, "Ray had a tap put on his home phone line! I wonder who was in charge of monitoring that... I'm sure going to find out!"

"I think someone needs to check on that property to see if that titanium really came from there."

"You got that thing right! I'll drive out there myself this afternoon."

I wasn't going to let this news screw up our Christmas. But I did need to check this out. The next few days our office would be closed till after New Years.

First, I called Larry and asked him if anything had turned up on the tap they had on Ray's phone. He assured me that it hadn't and told me that Joe Jenks was taking care of it personally. Yep, I had that one down pat!

At noon I just told Susan I was going out to lunch. I drove through Burger King and picked up a Whopper combo and headed out to the estate.

I had put up no trespassing signs right after the funeral. I went through the gate behind the mansion and followed the well-worn path through the old pasture out past the barn and into what was once the tobacco fields when it was being tended. Since Aunt Hazel had been so sick, Uncle Jake had let the farm grow up in grass and weeds. The quiet stream rambled off to my right. I knew that ore had come down some branches in Virginia and that titanium had been discovered and mined in the area, as well as other minerals.

I followed that picturesque stream, looking carefully in the water at the various colored stones which were rounded by countless years of the creek's flow. I walked very close to the bank and stared at the edges of the dark, rich soil. The recent snow had all melted and I had a great view of the land and the stream, known as Blair's Branch. There was not the slightest trace of any mineral there.

Their ploy had been a scam to solicit the help of those they needed. Zoning regulations would have made mining in the city limit impossible anyway. Obviously the folks involved were not lawyers! But just how deep was this quagmire? The ones being scammed could hardly take them to court after it was over.

I leisurely strolled back to my car and returned to my office to spend the rest of the business day shuffling papers.

Time to relax and enjoy our precious family.

Chapter 19

Christmas morning I woke up like a child who couldn't wait to see what Santa had brought. Annette was still asleep when I eased out of bed at 6:30.

What I was really anxious about was the fact that our whole family would be together that day.

Louisa came first with her fellow. By that time, 9:35, 'Nette was up and had coffee made.

Breakfast was on the table by the time Bobby got there at 10:22. His son Robert III, age 3, better known as Trey, and daughter, Desiree, 18 months, were both clinched in the hands of Bobby's wife, Missy.

Jonathan would naturally be the last arrival since they had to drive in from Matthews, North Carolina, a suburb of Charlotte. His frisky wife was Ashley, and they had but one boy, Manny, who was just a babe in arms.

We had a fantastic family and Annette and I loved every one of them to the moon and back. It was just a dirty shame that we couldn't get together more often.

Trey could hardly wait until we had eaten breakfast to open his gifts, but wait he must. The little ones were too young to realize the full impact of Christmas at the time, but seemed delighted to get new toys.

I know that children are spoiled with the latest of everything, and were even then. But they are only little once, we reasoned, so they would have what they wanted. We did teach them that they must be thankful, and that Jesus' birth was the reason for the Christmas celebration.

The adults in the family all shared gifts as well, and 'Nette and I waited until everyone else opened their gifts to do our own exchange. Our children respected the fact that we bought more for one another than for them. After all, all of them had their own family gift exchanges in their respective homes.

It was a delightful day and the babies shared their new playthings with one another and enjoyed rambling about in the special playroom that we had built into our home just for that purpose.

We listened to Christmas music and let the kids watch Rudolph and A Charlie Brown Christmas that evening.

Louisa and Bobby both drove home that night, but Jonny spent the night with us before starting home to North Carolina.

It was painful seeing each family leave, especially when Jonny, Ashley and Manny left the next morning; because we knew it would be months before we would get to see them again.

When Annette and I sat down after they left at 10:30, we felt like the wind had been knocked out of our sails and we were floating aimlessly on the salty sea of life.

But we had another whole week to collect ourselves before starting into 1992.

At least we thought we did.

Chapter 20

We were watching Dick Clark's New Year's Eve party on TV. Diverse beautiful fireworks were bursting into colorful blooms, not only on the show, but in the distance, downtown Roanoke at Market Square. The ball was just starting to drop on New York City when our front yard lit up like the full brilliance of the noonday sun!

I had begun to get drowsy in spite of all the noise; but now I was wide awake, for sure! I dashed into the living room and saw the fiery outline of a large flaming cross on our lawn! Quickly throwing the front door open, I could make out a shadowy figure jumping into a new Ford F150 and spinning tires out of our drive!

I grabbed the closest telephone and called Larry. It took three rings for him to answer and by that time I was worse than frantic.

"Not everyone stays up to see the New Year in, Rob! What the hell do you want at this hour of the night?"

"I can't prove who did this, but I just had a cross burned in my front yard! Now you know who is behind this, as sure as shooting!"

Larry swallowed hard.

"Go to bed, Rob!" Larry shouted in my ear. "There's nothing either of us can do tonight! What are they going to do as an encore?"

"If you and your cronies can't get his bunch of maniacs off my back I'll find a way to do it without you!"

"Now don't talk like that, Rob! You can't take the law into your own hands! You, of all people, know better than that! If something happens to any of Hazel's family I'll be coming after you! That would make them all happy as freakin' larks!"

"Just get on this pronto and let me know what you're doing."

"I'm not doing anything tonight! Let's both get some shut-eye."

So much for seeing the New Year in with a kiss. More like the kiss of death.

The next morning I called Barry and filled him in on what had happened.

He informed me that he was still having Patel tailed, but now he would be going after Joe Jenks as well.

Joe Jenks! I hadn't thought about tailing him. I had Ray Blair in mind. I didn't question him, though. I knew Barry was the hot shot investigator and he knew best. Perry Mason always trusted Paul Drake.

I got a call from Larry about 2:00 that afternoon and he told me that he had asked Jenks to put another officer on the trail of Jesse Henshaw and he was leaving Jenks on Ray.

Why did it always have to be Jenks? Obviously Larry didn't have a clue about Jenks' connections to the bad guys.

I still bit my tongue. Maybe it was a good thing; this way when Barry's man trailed Joe he would lead him to the source of the problem sooner than he had expected. He could kill two birds— or more—with one stone.

I was surprised again by a call from Barry that next Monday morning. I had been dead on the money. Jenks had gone straight to Henshaw and Ray. They had met at that same out-of-the-way restaurant where Ray had met Patel with the titanium ore, or whatever it was. Now we had proof of a true conspiracy involving an officer of the law.

I couldn't help but wonder though where the 'titanium' had come from and what Jenks had to gain by getting involved in this scam.

"Is it time to move, Barry?" I said.

"Not yet. We have a ways to go to get this wrapped up. I want a conclusive case against these scoundrels."

"You're the boss!"

"Thanks. You know I have to live up to my ad. I don't want you asking for your money back!"

I laughed.

"That's for sure. I'd rather pay you well than to end up on the losing end of this thing."

And boy was he right!

Chapter 21

It was Wednesday, January 22nd before I heard from Barry again. For some reason I wasn't getting anything from Larry at all. I decided that Barry was better than Larry anyway!

"Some developments have come up that I am going to have to check out personally. I'm coming over to Roanoke day after tomorrow. I'm not going to call you, though, until I have all my ducks in a row."

This was certainly unexpected, but welcome. He must be getting somewhere.

All day Friday I heard nothing. Saturday morning I was sitting home. The temperature had taken a nosedive again and I had just turned the thermostat up and set back down at the table with Annette when the phone rang.

"Hey, Rob, I'm not far from your house. Would you mind if I dropped by for a few minutes?"

"Of course not, Barry. I've been on pins and needles since you last called."

"See you in a bit."

I was standing at the door opening it before Barry got to my front stoop.

"Come in, my friend. You're going to freeze your butt off out there!"

"Nope! I'm not going to stay out here long enough for that!"

And he was in the door.

I called Annette to bring us two mugs of coffee. None of those tiny china cups on a morning like this.

We both sat down in the living room.

"I like your place out here, Rob. You have a very lovely home."

"Yeah, when I don't have Molotov cocktails landing in here or crosses burning on my lawn!"

Barry grinned.

"Well, I think we're ready to do something about that."

"Those words are music to my ears, my friend. What's the plan?"

"Of course you know we'll have to follow the right channels to see that justice is done. And once we legally prove that there is a conspiracy here involving Hazel's family we won't have to worry about their claim to the real estate."

"That's nice, but I'm more concerned about protecting Annette and me than that estate. The rest of our family hasn't been bugging me about it."

"Yes, but that estate is the reason that your family is in jeopardy."

"So what developments have come up and what can we do now?"

"Well, I checked further and found that Patel made a deposit of $5,000 on the day before your uncle died. That same day, $5,000 was deducted from Ray's savings."

"How were you able to get that information?"

"Oh, I have my connections. You can be sure that this is accurate. I believe that this was given as immediate earnest money and that he was promised a small percentage of the return on the titanium if the property was inherited by him and his brothers and sisters. He has two of each. That would mean that all of them were likely in on the scam."

"So what are you going to do?"

"I am going to present this information to Chief Watts and demand the arrest of everyone involved. I am going to ask him to charge Patel with first degree murder, and everyone else as accessories."

"Are you going to have him arrest Joe Jenks as well?"

"You bet your bottom dollar I am!"

Chapter 22

Early Monday morning Barry Black showed up at Roanoke Police Headquarters and asked to speak to Chief Larry Watts.

"And what is your name, sir?" the front desk sergeant, Lucile Sanchez, asked in a pithy tone.

"My name is Black, Barry Black. I'm a private investigator from Richmond."

"And what does this concern, Mr. Black?"

"My business is with Chief Watts, ma'am."

Lucy shrugged and frowned.

"I'll see if he will see you, Mr. Black. I know he has a busy day lined up."

"Tell him this is very important."

Lucy immediately dialed Larry's extension.

"Chief Watts said you can go on back. First door on the left down this hall."

Larry raised his head and glared into Barry's face.

"Black, is it? What can I do for you, sir?"

"I was hired by local attorney Robert Blair several weeks back to investigate the murder of his uncle. I know that you are a friend of Rob's and very familiar with this case. I appreciate everything you have done to help him sort out this baffling mystery. I know that your job is very demanding and that this is far from your only project."

"Well, thank you for that, Mr. Black," Larry nodded. A half grin coming to light on his face. "Yes, we do stay busy around here! But Rob hadn't said anything to me about hiring a private eye. I believe we are doing everything necessary to get to the bottom of what happened to Jake Blair."

"Rob was just frustrated and felt like he needed someone who could spend more time on this and who was from outside Roanoke County and could be fully objective."

"So what have you come up with that we don't already know?"

"You might be surprised, Chief. First of all, your county coroner, Dr. Patel, had problems before he left Richmond. I had reason to believe that he was capable of taking a life for pay. I had him tailed and he met with Hazel Blair's nephew, Ray, who was showing him a piece of ore. Then I found out through my confidential informants that $5,000 exchanged hands between Ray and Patel the day before Jake Blair was found dead in his cell. A private autopsy and blood test showed that Jake actually died of a drug that was put in his meal or drink that last night."

"Man, oh man! You have done some remarkable research, Black! Bravo!" Watts clapped his hands and threw his head back. "Now how are you going to prove this in court? And how did Patel get the drug into his food?"

"Again, you might be surprised. We have good evidence showing that Detective Joe Jenks is involved. We feel that he was most likely the one who got the drug into Jake's food."

"You can't prove a damn bit of this!"

"Oh yes I can, Chief! Now arrest these rascals and Jesse Henshaw before I call the Mayor and have you removed from office!"

Larry was turning red in the face. Before he could order Barry out, he left on his own accord and went directly to Rob's office.

"Wow! You told him that? You have more guts than I do!"

"Yeah, I guess. But I don't know him. And I don't have to live here! I'm not afraid of him."

About that time my direct line rang.

"Rob, I just had a visit from a smart aleck private investigator who says he works for you! Why did you go and get somebody from Richmond involved!"

"Because I know you're swamped. I'm glad I did, because you would have never investigated your buddy Jenks."

"I can't believe Joe had anything to do with this, Rob. I tell you what. I'm going to have Patel and Ray picked up. I won't do anything about Joe Jenks until I have some real evidence against him. Henshaw is already out on bail. We are already going to bring him to trial when the time is right. If we get any more charges, we can present them later. I know these guys will get out when they have a bail hearing."

"You do that. But you need to file charges against them for conspiracy to commit murder. We can make that stick. I will be in touch with the D.A.

Chapter 23

The District Attorney, Evelyn Brown, gave me no problem once Barry and I took in all the evidence we had assimilated. We got a court date set for Patel of April 20th. He would be first. We would work off of what was done in his case to try Ray and gather more evidence on Jenks.

Jury selection was done the week before the trial. Since Patel hadn't been in town but about a year and kept mostly to himself, it wasn't a problem to get impartial jurors.

The main courtroom was packed on that rainy Monday. Nothing was going to keep the gawkers away, because the local rag had given us a lot of coverage. We even had the local NBC affiliate, WSLS, Channel 10 on hand with reporters. Of course cameras were not allowed inside, but they had an excellent sketch artist there.

Trying a public official was big news.

"All rise! Court is now in session, the Honorable Judge Henry Parker presiding!"

I was sitting near the front wishing I was the one prosecuting Patel. Every eye was on the bench, every ear tuned in. Ray, Henshaw and Jenks had all been given subpoenas and were in the courtroom.

"Today is set for one and only one trial," Parker said. "The state versus Anand Patel, M.D. How do you plead, Dr. Patel?"

Max Bruner was on his feet.

"Not guilty, your honor!"

"Madam District Attorney, you may now present your case against Dr. Patel."

"Your honor, we have strong evidence showing that Dr. Patel did knowingly and with malice aforethought cause a dangerous drug to be placed in the food of city jail inmate, Jacob Blair, which did, without a doubt, lead to his demise. We further contend that this action was a part of a conspiracy by others for personal gain, and that Dr. Patel, at that time, was paid an immediate bribe of $5,000 with promise of future payments contingent on other gains by those involved."

There was a large sigh and a rumble in the courtroom. Dr. Patel looked visibly shaken.

"Are you ready to present your first witness, Ms. Brown?"

"I am, Your Honor. At this time I call Gerald Smithers to the stand."

"Please place your right hand on the Bible, Mr. Smithers. Do you swear to tell the truth, the whole truth and nothing but the truth, so help you God?"

"I do."

"Mr. Smithers, will you please take the stand?"

"On the night of December 22nd, 1991 did you follow Dr. Patel to the Night Owl Grill in Starkey?"

"I did."

"And did he meet someone there?"

"Yes, he met Ray Blair."

"Were you able to determine the purpose of that meeting?"

"Yes, ma'am, I was. Blair showed Patel a piece of ore about the size of his hand. I heard him say, 'Titanium.' Then I heard Patel plainly answer, 'I just had to see it for myself.'

"And what did you deduce from this?"

"I deduced that he was offering Patel a share of supposed proceeds for the sale of alleged mining of the titanium."

"Was there anything particular that made you feel this way?"

"There is a lot more to this story, Madam District Attorney, I'm going to let you call my boss, Barry Black. He also has some evidence to present."

"Thank you, Mr. Smithers; that will be all. You may be excused."

"I would like to call my next witness now. Mr. Barry Black, would you please come to the stand?"

After his swearing in, Evelyn Brown addressed him.

"Mr. Black, would you please tell me your involvement in this case?"

"Yes, ma'am. I am a private investigator out of Richmond. I have an unblemished record of reliable and honest investigations for the past eleven years. Last December, Your friend and fellow attorney, Rob Blair, hired me to investigate his uncle's mysterious death. Dr.

Patel had ruled Jake Blair's death as being from a myocardial infarction, commonly known as a heart attack. Because of the timing of his passing, the night before he was to go to trial for the alleged murder of his wife, Rob felt that there was something strange going on and asked his wife, a local physician to have an autopsy done. The autopsy and blood test showed that the 'heart attack' had been faked by placing a drug into his food the night he died. There were traces of the drug in his blood stream and in the contents of his stomach. Upon investigation, we found out that Dr. Patel had left his previous employment under suspicion of assisting a patient in a suicide. These factors caused us to dig deeper. We determined that Patel had received a large deposit immediately after both suspicious deaths."

"Your Honor," the D.A. said, "I would like to place in evidence a copy of Dr. Patel's bank statement subpoenaed to me from First National Bank, labeled prosecution exhibit number one, and a copy of a withdrawal made by Ray Blair from Watauga Bank earlier that day, labeled prosecution exhibit number two. And by the way, here is a picture given me by Mr. Black that Mr. Smithers took of Dr. Patel with Ray

Blair that night. I would like that to be labeled defense exhibit three."

The court officer took the exhibits and placed them in a row on the table in the front of the courtroom.

"And so, Mr. Black, do you have any idea who enabled the drug to get into Blair's food?"

"Yes, ma'am, we certainly do."

Chapter 24

"And just who do you contend was to blame for that?"

"We have good reason to believe that a detective with the local police department was responsible for placing the drug in Jake's food."

A thunderous gasp emitted from all around the courtroom. Jenks was fidgeting, but trying hard not to display his obvious anxiety.

"What makes you feel that way, Mr. Black? That's a very serious allegation to be making! To which detective are you referring, sir?"

"Detective Joseph Jenks, District Attorney Brown. Rob and I knew that someone in the department had to be involved, because though Dr. Patel had provided the drug, he hadn't been there the night of Mr. Blair's death.

"Jenks always found a way to be involved with the case. Because of his negative and indifferent attitude toward the investigation, Rob Blair got suspicious and asked me to have my assistant, Gerald Smithers, tail him. Jenks met with Ray Blair and Jesse Henshaw, who had already been arrested for threatening Rob, at the same little restaurant where Ray had met with Patel.

The cook at the jail, Kerry Crane, is here and prepared to testify that Jenks personally asked him to take Blair's meal back to him that night!"

Jenks jumped and bolted for the door. The officers of the court rushed him and grabbed him before he could get away.

"Chief Watts, would you please take your detective into custody!" the judge snapped.

Larry had a cold, blank look on his face as he cuffed Jenks and asked Captain Doug Showalter to read him his rights and take him to lock up.

As Joe Jenks was taken away, he scowled and glowered back at Larry.

"You better see that I get the best attorney in Roanoke, Chief!"

I smiled. I considered that to be me, and there was not 'a snowball's chance in hell' of him getting me!

"I know that there are others being charged in this conspiracy. Can you tell me who they are and what charges you're making?"

"Yes, ma'am. Ray Blair, Jesse Henshaw, and of course Detective Jenks. There may be others, but I don't wish to say at the moment because I am still in the employ of Rob Blair and the investigation is ongoing."

"Thank you, Mr. Black, you may be excused."

"Since it is almost 12:00 o'clock, we will break for lunch," Judge Parker said. "Court is adjourned until 1:30 this afternoon!" And the sound of the heavy gavel on the bench rang throughout the large courtroom.

Chapter 25

I had lunch with Barry at Macado's, a nostalgic restaurant downtown with great ambiance. They had been in business there since 1978, and I enjoyed their menu choices. I had boneless wings and I don't remember what he had; it's just been too long ago. I just know I ordered the wings because they were my favorite lunch item and were fast to get.

I told him what a jam-up job he was doing. He had even surprised me with some of the evidence he had been able to obtain. I just left it in his capable hands.

"Do you have any more witnesses?" I asked.

"None that I will need to call now that they have taken Jenks into custody. I have some other thoughts on this, but we are only trying Patel right now, and we have him dead to rights."

When we got back and everyone was seated I moved my eyes around the courtroom. Ray and

Henshaw were missing. Hmm. Who had given them the option of leaving?

"All rise!"

I turned and saw that Judge Parker was there in all of his glory.

"Madam District Attorney, do you have any other witnesses?"

"I was going to call Ray Blair. He is a hostile witness, but he had a subpoena. He was here earlier. Since he is out on bail and was here at my request, I ask that a bench warrant be issued for his arrest."

"Bailiff, would you see that this is done and that Mr. Blair is picked up forthwith, please?"

"Yes, Your Honor!"

"Anyone else, Ms. Brown?"

"No, Your Honor. I rest my case."

"Mr. Bruner, you may call your first witness."

Max Bruner was visibly confused. He had also sent Ray a subpoena the day before not knowing that he had already received one to testify for the D.A.

"Your honor, I am without witnesses. I had Detective Jenks and Ray Blair lined up. I had not been informed of the alleged involvement of these gentlemen in this case."

"Thank you Mr. Bruner. I am going to turn this over to the jury at this time."

It took the jury less than 90 minutes to deliver a guilty verdict.

I gave Barry a big hug and thanked him very sincerely.

"Just wait until you get my final bill! Thank you for putting your confidence in me! But now we have some more scoundrels to put away!

"Right you are! But I feel useless as an attorney."

"Don't worry. You'll be on the witness stand before this is over. Ray is next. I'm going to let Jenks stew for a bit.

Chapter 26

I was a little uneasy about letting Jenks set, but I asked the D.A. to file an injunction to disallow bail for him due to his position and the seriousness of his charges. Conspiracy to commit murder and now, first degree murder; plus use of his office for illegal personal gain. I figured that he was just as guilty of murder as Patel because he had allegedly given my uncle the fatal drug. The injunction was accepted and he would remain incarcerated until his day in court.

Barry convinced me to go after Ray for conspiracy to commit murder, offering a bribe for criminal intent and personal gain, and lying to an officer of the law.

I was sure that he was guilty of even more, but this was enough to put him away for many years.

The sentencing hearing for the 'good doctor' came up in late May and he was given life in prison without the possibility of parole. At least he would play the devil trying to kill anyone else.

Ray's trial was set for June 29th and Barry had been busy collecting additional evidence.

He found a neighbor of Uncle Jake's that had seen Ray going through the gate leading to the back of the estate not long after the murder and had seen him coming out about two hours later with a 'rock' in his hand.

Could it be that the ore actually came from that place? What were the implications of this?

I called a representative with U.S. Mining Company and had him send out a couple of experts in locating and identifying ore.

Their search located traces of titanium which they said had floated downstream from a previous mining operation in a neighboring county.

Mystery solved.

On the first anniversary of Aunt Hazel's death I sat out on our patio and watched the strawberry moon rise on the eastern horizon over a small row of white pines which I had had planted between our house and our nearest neighbor to the east. There was a depressing and empty feeling as those memories of a year before flooded over my soul. I didn't stay out long after that. I went inside and gave Annette a gripping hug.

"What's that all about?" she said.

"It's a sad time, Honey. Do you know what tonight is?"

She thought a minute and sighed, returning my hug. Yes, she knew.

Ray's jury selection was slower than anticipated and delayed the actual start of the trial by a full week and one day. There was the Fourth of July holiday in there, too.

We all gathered in the courthouse on July 7th and the first gavel was at 9:30 AM.

By that time, the weather was heating up drastically and the air conditioning in the huge courtroom was going on and off. They had decided to open the windows.

Everyone was seated at least 15 minutes early. It seemed that the whole county expected a giant circus show that day. The first trial had caused such a stir that people from as far away as

Richmond and Wytheville had showed up and a whole bus load from Montgomery County; some from Christiansburg, some from Blacksburg. It had been difficult for many folks to find a parking place. Luckily, I had a reserved one in the court square.

This time both the NBC and CBS affiliates were on hand. The Today Show people were even there!

Everything went like clockwork. We didn't have to worry about the members of the triad involved being present and accounted for. Patel would not be on hand because he was already serving his sentence and had nothing to gain by testifying against his co-conspirator. But Jenks, who was in police custody and Henshaw, who had been picked up and taken in cuffed, were certainly on hand.

The judge opened by calling up the D.A. to state her case and start bringing up her witnesses.

She first rehashed the findings presented in the Patel trial and stated the charges which had been leveled against Ray.

I could see that his two brothers were setting on the second row in the front, on the right side next to the center aisle. I knew who they were because I had seen pictures of them at Uncle Jake and Aunt Hazel's house and the youngest one, John, was almost a twin to Ray.

Ms. Brown's first witness was none other than yours truly.

"Mr. Blair, you are a very distinguished and trusted attorney here in Roanoke. Isn't Ray Blair related to you?"

"Yes, ma'am, very distantly. He is my fourth cousin."

"But isn't there another relationship due to marriage?"

"Yes, ma'am. Ray's late father was a brother of my deceased aunt by marriage."

"Would that make him a first cousin by marriage?"

"Not really," I mumbled. "But we are both her nephews." *Why would she say something like that?*

"Exactly what do you believe drove your *cousin* to the crime for which he is being charged? And what would he have to gain?"

"My uncle and aunt died intestate. For those who may not be familiar with this legal term, this means that they didn't have wills. They owned their property as Tenants of the Entirety. They chose not to have me draw up wills for them, in spite of my insistence that I do so, because Virginia estate law passes on all real estate and personal property to the surviving spouse when one dies."

"But something unusual happened here, didn't it, Mr. Blair?"

"Yes, ma'am. It did. My aunt died unexpectedly and because of unusual circumstances, my uncle was charged with murdering her. Under the law if someone murders another, he or she may not inherit any property from them.

I was preparing his defense, in which I had sufficient information to clear him of the charge against him.

"Ray and his two brothers and two sisters felt that he was her killer and that the property should go to them—lock, stock and barrel. When they got nervous as to the possibility of my uncle's being cleared of murder, they took the matter into their own hands and conspired with Dr. Patel to make sure he didn't live to be cleared. Dr. Patel then enlisted Joe Jenks, a police detective, to help him kill my uncle and make it appear to be a heart attack. Dr. Patel has already been convicted and is serving a life sentence for this murder. We will be trying Detective Jenks later this year."

"Thank you, Mr. Blair. I know this has been, and will continue to be, stressful on you."

The D. A. turned it over to James Brinkley, Ray's attorney. He had no further questions for me, of course.

Brinkley first called Ray's brother, Sam, as a character witness. Sam swore under oath that he was close to his brother and that the charges were unfounded. Since Ray's wife had been visiting with her sister, he could not prove his whereabouts on the night he had supposedly met with Patel at the Night Owl Grill in Starkey, but John had told Sam that he had been with him there that night.

Then Brinkley called up John who stated that he had indeed been at the restaurant with his brother on the night in question and that he had no contact with Patel. After John's testimony, Judge Parker turned over the witness to D.A. Brown.

"That has been quite a while back, Mr. Blair. How can you be sure it was that night?"

"Because we go there every Sunday night!"

"Why would Gerald Smithers, the investigator who testified in Patel's trial, have made this up? We have a picture in evidence from Patel's trial that we can bring back out. Do we need to do that, Mr. Blair?"

"Rob made it up because he wants his family to get my aunt's property! That picture could have been faked! They can do almost anything on computers now, I've heard."

There was a roar which echoed through the entire second floor of the crowded, overheated courthouse.

"Motion to strike, your honor!" Evelyn Brown said in a firm, raised voice.

"Unless you have someone to witness your claim that you were there that night, Mr. Blair, I am going to have the jury disallow it!" the judge snarled.

John Blair was silent.

"So moved!" said the judge.

Once the testimonies and final statements had been made, the jury was ordered to their room to deliberate the verdict.

One juror was uncertain and made all sorts of objections, I was later told. But after two hours and ten minutes they announced that they had reached a verdict.

Guilty on all counts.

Chapter 27

I had just gotten into my office the next morning after the trial when my intercom went off. Since my mind was elsewhere it alarmed me.

"Call for you on line one, Rob. Some lady from the police department."

"Thanks, Susan."

"Hi Rob. This is Lucy Sanchez. Joe Jenks wants to see you. He told me last night to have you come over here this morning as soon as you can.

Her tone was hushed and concerned. Rob could tell that the sergeant was trying not to be heard by someone who must not be far away.

"See me? Why on God's green earth would Jenks want to see me? I have absolutely nothing to say to that man!"

"But he has something to say to you, Rob. He says it's urgent! You will want to hear him out."

I twisted my mouth to one side and frowned.

"This had better be good! I'll be heading over there in about forty-five minutes. I have a phone interview with a potential client in ten minutes."

When I got to the station, Lucy motioned for me to go on back. As I passed Larry's office, the door was open and the Chief threw up his hand and said good morning.

No one from outside had gone into the jail yet that morning, as breakfast was running late, and I had to get Showalter to let me in.

Jenks' cell was in the very back of the dark hall. The 10 X 10 cells were all on one side on that wing and no one was in the adjoining chamber. When I got there, Joe Jenks' limp body was hanging by a bed sheet from the ceiling of his cubical!

"Showalter! I screamed. Get Larry fast! Jenks is dead!"

Larry came flying in like a stream of bullets from an AR15!

"What the bloody hell?"

"Now how do you suppose this happened? This is the second mysterious death in *your* jail this year!"

"Yeah, but the other one was caused by Jenks. He must have not wanted to go to trial and chose to end it all to prevent the embarrassment of being found guilty."

I shook my head, but I kept my tongue in my mouth. Something wasn't jiving and I was afraid to say anything till I had more information.

It seemed like longer, but it must have been only about thirty seconds later when I answered.

"What a shame, Larry! We may never get to the bottom of everyone involved in this awful plot!"

"I really think we have everybody. I know Joe's wife pretty well. I'll let her know what has happened. There is nothing you can do here now. I heard that Joe wanted to talk to you about something. Do you have any idea what he wanted?"

"I don't have the foggiest notion, Larry."

Larry sighed.

"I guess we'll never know now. He must have decided he didn't really need to talk to you before he hanged himself."

What? I thought. *He's going to automatically assume that Joe took his own life.*

Luckily I was a good friend of the new coroner, Dr. Nate Argo. As soon as I got back to my office I told Susan and Allen about the weird turn of events and got on the horn with Nate. I explained to him that he was about to be called to pronounce Joe Jenks dead. He said that he was on the way out the door because he had already received the call. Larry had phoned him and told him that he had talked with Rosie Jenks, the widow, and she wanted to have him taken directly to the funeral home. She planned, he said, on cremation.

I told Nate that he needed to examine the body to determine if death had been caused by hanging or not. He seemed perplexed, but knowing me, and the fact that I was involved with the case against Jenks, agreed to do it for my sake.

I told him to record his findings and be prepared to give them in court later if needed. I still didn't know where I was going with this, but was confident that I was taking the right first step.

Chapter 28

Even before I got the call from Nate, which was of itself revealing, I heard from Desk Sergeant Lucy Sanchez.

"Rob, I'm at lunch. I left early so I could catch you before you went out. I had to wait till I got away from the office to call you. I don't want to tell you this on the phone. Could you meet me over here? I'm at Alexander's on Jefferson. I came here because I knew no one else from our office eats here."

"Sure, I know where it is. Be there in a jiffy."

She had ordered blackened salmon and it looked so delicious that I told our waiter that I wanted the same thing.

Annette and I had never gone there, and I decided that day to put Alexander's on our list of evening dining spots, though I knew dinner required a reservation.

"Well, Rob, I don't think you are ready for this. I know you and Larry are old friends."

My brows went up.

"Yes, but he has been acting awfully strange since this whole mess started. Are you trying to tell me that Larry is in some way involved in the death of my uncle?"

"Well, let's start at the first. You may know that Larry and his wife Ann divorced over a year ago,"

"That's hardly news. Of course. I never tried to get involved in anyone else's marital affairs. I thought Larry may have a girl friend, but I was afraid to say anything."

"As a matter of fact he did...does. He has been having an affair with Rosie Jenks since before the divorce."

"My Lord! No!"

"Yes. He has no idea that I'm aware of it. But a few days ago Jenks found out about the affair. I won't tell you how he found out, but he did."

"Well, you knew about it. Just be honest with me, Lucy. Did you tell him?"

Lucy broke out in tears.

"It's alright, Luce. Just tell me what happened."

"I feel responsible for his death. I have had feelings for Joe since right after I found out his wife was cheating on him with the Chief. I wanted so badly to tell him but dared not to. I would go back and visit Joe in his cell when Larry was out to lunch. He told me that Larry had told him to take the food back to your uncle that night he died. He told me that it was Larry who placed the drug in it, not him. That's why he wanted to see you. He wanted you to defend him.

"Showalter heard him say that he was going to ask you to defend him and told Larry. That's how Joe ended up dead."

"But why in heaven's name would Larry get involved with this?"

"I have no idea, Rob."

I just shook my head and thanked Lucy. When I got back to my office I had a message on my answering machine to call Nate.

Chapter 29

"**W**ell, Rob, you're going to be surprised by what I found. Death was by asphyxiation, not from that bed sheet Jenks was hanging by!"

"Doesn't surprise me in the least, Nate."

"It appears that he was smothered, likely by his pillow, so there would be no commotion for the other prisoners to hear. Whoever did this performed the act while Jenks was sleeping."

"Do you have any idea who could have done this? It had to be someone on the police force."

"Yes, Nate, I'm afraid I do. But let me put a case together before I let the cat out of the bag."

It was the next morning before I got a call from Larry asking me to meet him out at Uncle Jake's place. He said he had a line on the origin of the titanium and what should be done before our family sold the estate.

Of course that dead skunk stunk to high heaven. Larry had found out somehow that I was wise to him and had some sinister plan up his sleeve. I called the front desk back and Lucy answered. I told her not to say anything that could alert Larry in case he was listening around the corner. I told her that I was meeting the Chief at Uncle Jake's in thirty minutes. I asked her to do what she thought was necessary. I knew that she wouldn't let me down.

I met Larry in front of the main gate and we walked up together. He said that we needed to go in the house. I knew there was a method to his madness, but I complied. Once inside, I could smell a stifling odor. I knew it was kerosene and started edging toward the door.

As I neared the closed exit, Larry said loudly, "I wouldn't do that if I were you!"

I whirled around to see his .38 revolver starring me in the eye from eight feet away!

"Now, Larry, you know better than to do this! What are you going to gain?"

"I am going to avoid the charges that you intend to file against me. You know what I did, and I will never see the life I have planned with Rosie!"

"But why, Larry? How did you get into this mess? You have a clean record as police chief here for the past five years!"

"You might as well know. You won't be telling anyone else anyway! Rosie is a dear friend of Maggie Blair, Ray's wife. They were best friends in high school. Maggie told Rosie that they were going to be inheriting this place and that it had titanium on it and that they needed me to make sure your murdering uncle died before he came to trial. They promised me a one percent return on the titanium. They told me that they had talked to the city zoning board about a method of mining it that would not disturb anyone."

"Now that you have seen that my patsy, Jenks, was convicted for the murder, and now that I have made sure he won't rat me out, since there is no way to get paid on the titanium anyway, I am going to get rid of this house and you with it!"

"But Larry! There is no real vein of titanium here anyway! I had the mining company check it out!"

"Doesn't matter to me, Rob! At least Rosie and I can have a life together and put this all behind us."

I had nothing to lose. And nobody had apparently come to see about us. I quickly grabbed a heavy framed picture from the wall by the door and hurled it at Larry. He ducked and a shot rang out from his revolver in my direction. The picture grazing his head had stunned him.

The shot hit below my left shoulder just above my heart. I fell motionless to the floor.

Larry spun around, lit a match and tossed it onto the kerosene soaked carpet. Flames jumped high in the room as Larry dashed for the door.

Before he could get over my body on the floor, the door flew open. It was Lieutenant Ben Kirk, a highly decorated African American officer with an impeccable record of nine years service.

Right behind him were Lieutenant Doug Showalter and Sergeant Lucy Sanchez. Showalter cuffed Watts while Kirk picked me up and got me out, placing a piece of my shirt which he had torn off against the wound on my shoulder as Lucy called 9-1-1.

Lucy had waited until Larry had left the building and briefed Lieutenants Doug Showalter and Ben Kirk about mine and Larry's meeting and that there may be trouble. She asked them to take her in a patrol car to join us, giving them details of our situation on the way out.

Behind us, the striking remainder of Old Colonial Virginia burned to the ground in spite of the heroic efforts of the Roanoke Fire Department.

Chapter 30

Afterward

Needless to say, Chief Larry Watts was convicted of first degree murder and sentenced to death in the electric chair. The good folks of Roanoke were sick and tired of corruption in law enforcement. The state has now abolished the death penalty, but this was several years too late to save Watts.

Ben Kirk was overwhelmingly elected as the new chief right after Watts was jailed. He made an excellent chief.

Rosie Jenks cried her pretty little eyes out. Chief Watts stayed on death row for fifteen years and was denied a new trial on two separate occasions. His sentence was finally carried out and Rosie has since remarried.

Jesse Henshaw, Ray Blair and his younger brother, John, were all convicted of conspiracy to commit murder. Henshaw was sentenced to ten years in prison, as was Ray Blair. John got eight. All three served their entire sentences and are now out. None of them have had any other scrapes with the law. But Jesse has been watched closely for illegal clan activities. I guess they all came to realize that there are dire consequences for greed.

In 1994 our family put ReMax in charge of selling the estate and they subdivided it into three sections. The two smaller plots, facing main road, where the mansion had stood, sold to a major hotel chain and for a large truck stop. The other 100 acres plus was purchased by a developer who built a gated community with a private tennis court and nine hole golf course.

Even without the old mansion, the property brought considerably more than anticipated.

Just before Uncle Jake's estate was broken up and sold, my father died of a heart attack and his share of the estate was passed on to Liz and me. With my portion, I set up a trust fund for my grandchildren to pay for their college.

Robert II, whom we call Bobby, divorced in 2002, and their children stayed with their mother in Vinton. He moved to Los Angeles to manage an upper class restaurant which he ended up buying when the owner retired. He never remarried but "enjoys the carefree life of a bachelor," in his words, with a beachfront home in Malibu. He's too far away, and I rarely get to see him, but Missy was great to allow us time with Trey and Desiree when they were growing up. Without their father there, they have been cheated of that influence and guidance. Desiree went on to college at Hollins University and became a nurse practitioner.

Trey got in with bad company and ended up on drugs. Bobby has been so far away that Trey blamed his problems on his absentee father. I have done all I knew how to do for him, but he is still in and out of the wrong company.

Louisa and her fiancé broke up after one year as a couple, and she went on to college at Virginia Tech. She watched the massacre that took place there in 2007 on television with horror and was super glad that she had graduated ten years earlier.

She married a lawyer named Matt Price in Charlottesville two years after graduation. I guess girls really do look for someone who reminds them of their father. She decided to be a paralegal and work in the firm where he was employed. They have two fine daughters who took advantage of their college funds.

Jonathan stayed happily married to Ashley and is still employed in banking, and is the COO of a large bank in Charlotte, North Carolina. His family moved into a new development much like the one built on Jake's old farm years ago.

They had one more boy whom they named Jacob after my dear uncle. They thought that was the least they could do to show their appreciation for the school fund which had come from his estate. Luckily, both of Jonny's boys went on to college at UNC there in Charlotte.

I have now told my children about my terminal tumor, and though they are very distraught, they have come to accept the fact that I won't be with them much longer and that I have given everything over to God.

Yes, that's the story I've been struggling with for thirty years.

So, rest in peace Uncle Jake and Aunt Hazel. I will soon be joining you.

All's well that ends well.
I've decided not to tell

what I saw that fateful night in June
by the glow of the strawberry moon.

About the Author

Stanley J. "Stan" St. Clair is a newspaper columnist for **The Southern Standard** and **The Smithville Review**, and the author of more than 25 other published books including the critically acclaimed series **Most Comprehensive Origins of Clichés, Proverbs and Figurative Expressions.**

He is also the sole owner of St. Clair Publications at http://stclairpublications.com. His articles and nostalgic poems have been published in numerous newspapers, magazines and books in the U.S., Canada and the U.K., and on several websites.

Stan served as a State Commissioner of the Scottish Clan Sinclair, U.S.A.; first for Georgia, then Tennessee, for several years and as its Eastern Vice President for two years. He was a regular contributor to their official publication **Yours Aye** for a number of years.

He has also been a member of Kiwanis International since 1984, and has served in every position in his local club including several terms as president, and one year as District Lieutenant Governor.

Stan was knighted in 2003. He is an active Turcopolier in the OSMTJ - Knights Templar Grand Priory of America, Priory of the Risen King, and the Commandant of the Commandery of St. Francis.

He studied creative writing at Tennessee State University and holds a BRE degree from Covington Theological Seminary. He was awarded an honorary PhD in 2020.

He is also the co-founder of St. Clair Research, which may be viewed on the Internet at http://www.stclairresearch.com with his distant cousin, Ad Exec Steve St. Clair, who owns and manages the project.

Stan was selected for inclusion in the 2022 *Marquis' Who's Who in America*.

Stan and his wife, Rhonda, live in Tennessee.

www.ingramcontent.com/pod-product-compliance
Lightning Source LLC
Chambersburg PA
CBHW050824180626
46814CB00004B/1445